For August and Tallulah, Ann, G (and Sass + Sunny),
our life-long friends and help-line

DIAL BOOKS FOR YOUNG READERS
A division of Penguin Young Readers Group
Published by The Penguin Group
Penguin Group (USA) Inc., 375 Hudson Street, New York, NY 10014, U.S.A.
Penguin Group (Canada), 90 Eglinton Avenue East, Suite 700, Toronto,
Ontario, Canada M4P 2Y3 (a division of Pearson Penguin Canada Inc.)
Penguin Books Ltd, 80 Strand, London WC2R 0RL, England
Penguin Ireland, 25 St. Stephen's Green, Dublin 2, Ireland (a division of Penguin Books Ltd)
Penguin Group (Australia), 250 Camberwell Road, Camberwell, Victoria 3124, Australia
(a division of Pearson Australia Group Pty Ltd)
Penguin Books India Pvt Ltd, 11 Community Centre, Panchsheel Park, New Delhi - 110 017, India
Penguin Group (NZ), 67 Apollo Drive, Rosedale, Auckland 0632, New Zealand
(a division of Pearson New Zealand Ltd)
Penguin Books (South Africa) (Pty) Ltd, 24 Sturdee Avenue,
Rosebank, Johannesburg 2196, South Africa
Penguin Books Ltd, Registered Offices: 80 Strand, London WC2R 0RL, England

The publisher does not have any control over and does not assume any
responsibility for author or third-party websites or their content.

Designed by Jasmin Rubero
Text set in Museo Slab 500

Manufactured in China on acid-free paper

10 9 8 7 6 5 4 3 2 1

Library of Congress Cataloging-in-Publication Data
Soman, David.
The amazing adventures of Bumblebee Boy / by David Soman and Jacky Davis.
p   cm.
Summary: As imaginary superhero Bumblebee Boy, Sam rejects his pesky little brother's help
in defeating pirates, dragons, and saber-toothed lions, but when Sam comes up against
some scary aliens, he discovers the advantage of having a sidekick.
ISBN 978-0-8037-3418-0 (hardcover)
[1. Play—Fiction. 2. Imagination—Fiction. 3. Superheroes—Fiction. 4. Brothers—Fiction.]
I. Davis, Jacky, date. II. Title.
PZ7.S696224Am 2011
[E]—dc22
2011004567

THE **AMAZING ADVENTURES** OF
BUMBLEBEE BOY

by *David Soman* and *Jacky Davis*

Dial Books for Young Readers an imprint of Penguin Group (USA) Inc.

BUM Ba BUM BUMM!

Sam is
BUMBLEBEE BOY!

Oh no! GREENBEARD the Evil Pirate
is trying to get *BUMBLEBEE BOY!*

He has a big sword, but *BUMBLEBEE BOY* isn't afraid!

BUMBLEBEE BOY aims his stinger . . .

"I can play too?" asks Owen.

Owen is Sam's brother.

He always wants to play what Sam is playing.

"No, Owen! I am playing **_BUMBLEBEE BOY_**," says Sam.

"You can't be in this game."

"Why?" asks Owen.

This is a bit of a problem. Sam knows that he is not supposed to
be mean to Owen, but he feels like playing his own game right now.

Sam must think fast.

"Because," says Sam, "you are not a superhero like me, see?"

Sam dashes off.

Today **BUMBLEBEE BOY** flies alone!

BUM Ba BUM BUMM!

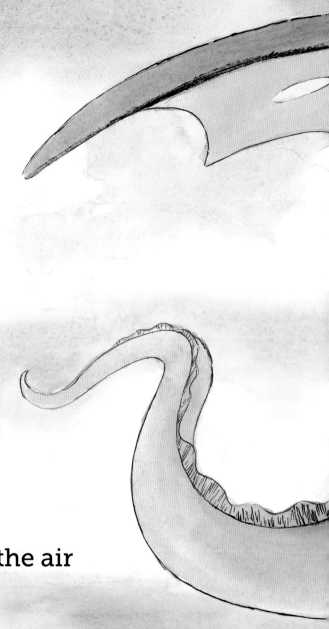

BUMBLEBEE BOY is flying through the air

and sees his enemy

FIRE DRAGON!

Fire Dragon tries to blast him with his Fire Breath,

but **BUMBLEBEE BOY** is too fast!

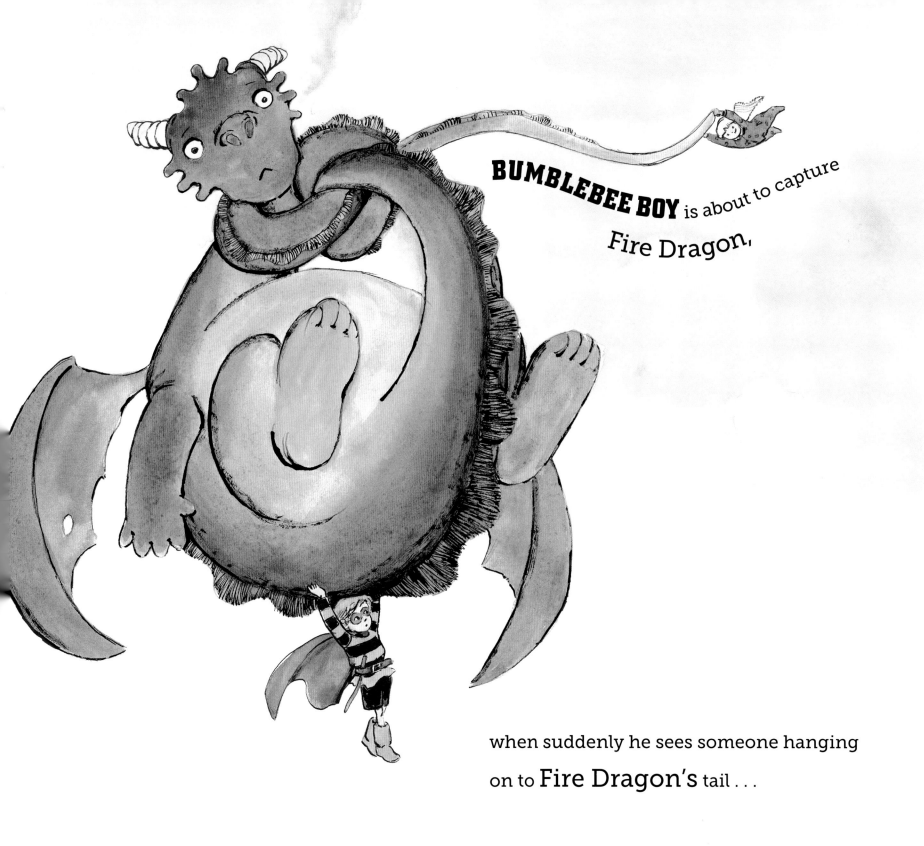

BUMBLEBEE BOY is about to capture
Fire Dragon,

when suddenly he sees someone hanging
on to **Fire Dragon's** tail . . .

"I play now? I can fly too?"

It is Owen again. He has a cape.

"Stop bothering me, Owen!" says Sam.

"But I am soup hero too!" says Owen.

"Owen," explains Sam patiently, "you only have a cape.

A cape is not enough to be a superhero."

Owen still doesn't get it;

BUMBLEBEE BOY wants to fly alone!

BUM Ba BUM BUMM!

BUMBLEBEE BOY is at the circus when suddenly **GIGANTO,** the Giant Saber-Toothed Lion, breaks his chain.

He wants to eat the whole audience!

BUMBLEBEE BOY will have to stop him!

But is he too wild for **BUMBLEBEE BOY**? Giganto has long teeth and claws.

What a battle!

Who will win?

Wait a minute.

Giganto is rolling over on his back.

Someone is rubbing his tummy . . .

"I tame Giganto too! I am soup hero too, see? I have mask!" says Owen.

"That's not a mask," says Sam, "that's a hat! It is for being outside! If you go outside, I will play with you later, okay?"

"I want to fight Giganto with you!" says Owen.

"Well, I don't feel like fighting Giganto anymore," says Sam. "You can go and fight him by yourself."

In this game,

BUMBLEBEE BOY flies alone!

But **BUMBLEBEE BOY** is driving
the Beemobile.

He drives fast, but so do the bank robbers.
BUMBLEBEE BOY cannot catch them!
It looks like they are going to escape!
Suddenly, another car cuts them off! Hooray!
The bank robbers will be captured!

Owen. Owen has a box.

"I have car too!" says Owen. "I can play now?"

Sam has to think.

It was kind of fun when Owen helped catch the bank robbers,

but Sam is still not sure if he is ready to play with anybody else.

"I know," says Sam. "You can play in your box . . . in here."

BUM Ba Bum BUMM!

BUMBLEBEE BOY

is exploring the moon!

Suddenly a bunch of scary and tough-looking **ALIENS** come to capture him!

BUMBLEBEE BOY realizes that he will never be able to
defeat so many by himself!

He needs help!

He needs a partner.

He needs . . .

Sam knows who he needs.

"Do you want to play **BUMBLEBEE BOY** with me?" asks Sam. "I'm fighting aliens!"

"No, I don't want to fight aliens," says Owen. "Am playing bank robber monsters."

"Bank robber monsters," says Sam. "What game is that?"

"Is this!" says Owen.

"Oh," says Sam.

He thinks for a minute.

"You know, Owen," says Sam, "there are bank robber
monsters in fighting aliens too."

"Really?" says Owen.

"Yes," says Sam. "So will you come fight aliens with me?"

"BUM Ba BUM BUMM!!!!" yells Owen.

After all, thinks Sam, ***BUMBLEBEE BOY*** flies alone . . .

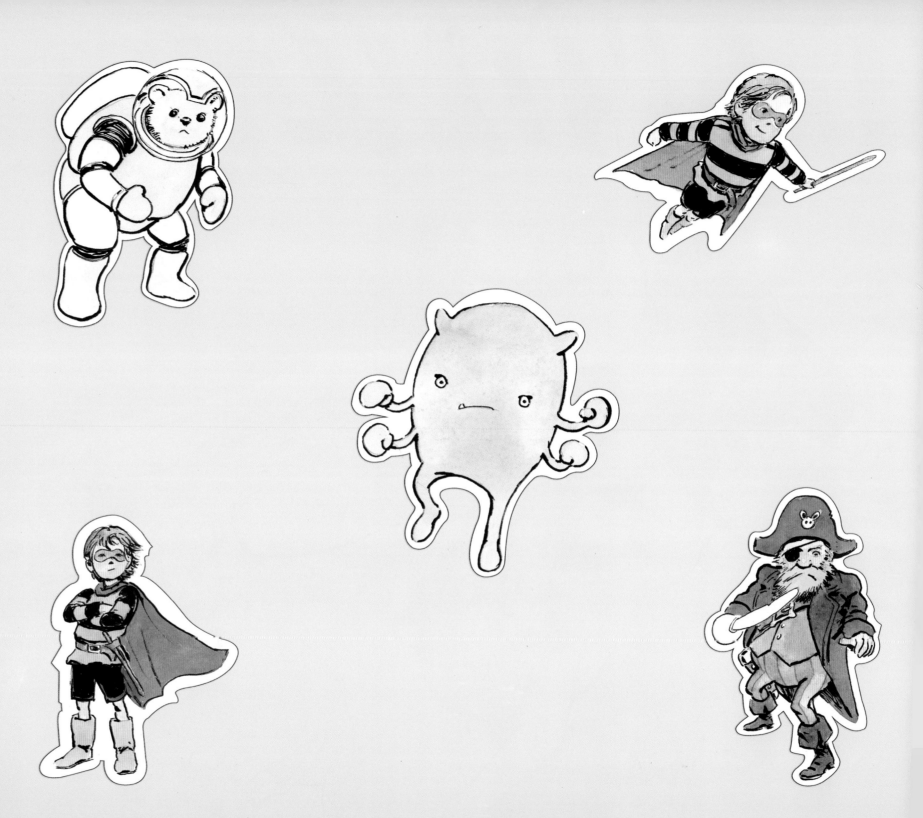